Kateryna Babkina

Cappy and the Whale

Translated by
Hanna Leliv

Illustrated by
Julia Pylypchatina

PUFFIN

To my mother, to Bohdan when he was little,
and to Tanya Shapochka, Maria and Dasha
and everyone who is fighting

THE WHALE WHO EATS MY PILLS

One morning I glanced out of the window and saw a whale floating in the sky. The whale was blue and grey, large and clumsy, yet he was just rolling along and gliding on the warm sunny breeze with surprising grace.

I grabbed Mum's phone from her desk to take a picture, but the whale arched his back and dived into the treetops, through the early spring leaves. Small birds fluttered up, chirping angrily.

While I was in the hospital, I read every book in the world about animals. Well, not *every* book – it was actually twenty-three, but that's still a lot. I read about this fish that can crawl on land during droughts, about the platypus that digs a burrow underwater, and about the monster living at the bottom of Loch Ness in Scotland. And about the fifty-two different types of flying fish that have fins big enough for them to speed up and leap out of the water and glide over the waves. But none of these books mentioned a whale being able to swim in the air, high up above the park, in the late afternoon.

That evening, Grandma took me out for a walk. I looked and looked into the green gloom of the early night sky, the darkness tangled up in the rustling bushes, until I felt dizzy. Grandma got scared – she thought I'd grown weak again and had fallen asleep standing up. But I couldn't help staring up at the treetops, trying to catch a glimpse of the huge whale up there, moving around, hiding, breathing in and out.

When we got home, Grandma fussed around trying to take my clothes off so she could check my body for new bruises, but I hate that – I'm not a little boy any more. Before I went to the hospital last year, I broke my swimming coach's nose when he tried to help me hurry up and change into my swimming trunks by pulling off my underpants. He kept shaking his head and laughing at me as he wiped away the blood. I was in no laughing mood, though, because I couldn't stop thinking about what Mum was going to say. When the coach told my mum what had happened, she listened carefully, and then, after a long, silent drive home, she said to me, 'Adults should never take off your clothes or touch you in a way that feels uncomfortable. But if they do – like when Grandpa pinches your nose – there's no need to punch them. In fact, you shouldn't punch *anyone*.' But then, after she'd thought about it a bit more, she added, 'But actually you did everything right.'

So then I had even less idea what to think!

The coach and I had a talk, man to man. We agreed that he would never touch my underpants again and that I wouldn't touch his nose. Then he gave me a small hourglass to keep in my locker. It measured time: I had exactly three minutes to change into my swimming trunks.

Every time Mum took me to the locker room, she'd see the hourglass and remember the broken nose and laugh. Later, my coach brought me that hourglass while I was in the hospital, but that time Mum burst into tears. There's nothing scarier than seeing Mum cry, when blue-black tears run down her face. I'm not scared because of the blue-black – I know it's only make-up. I get scared because she seems to shrink when she's crying. She grows smaller than me, becoming so tiny and fragile that I don't know what to do with her or how to protect her. I'm OK when Mum gets angry, though, because she grows big then – big and angry and strong. I'm glad that Mum didn't cry or yell at me when I punched my coach. I think he liked her. I'm sad I stopped going to the pool.

So anyway – back with Grandma . . . I went to the bathroom alone and took off everything I was wearing except my underpants, and checked my arms, my shins, my bottom and my back in the mirror. I didn't see any bruises. When you get bruises like mine, you don't feel good. You can barely keep your eyes open, and if you hold your breath and blow all the air out and squint slowly, it feels like you'll become so light that you could fly right up off the ground. That never actually happened to me, though. I just fell down: once back in kindergarten and one time in the locker room at the swimming pool. That was when Coach saw all my bruises.

Grandma was waiting for me behind the door. I told her I was all right but that I wanted to be alone, so she went back to the kitchen, and I plugged the drain and started to fill the bathtub. I had to think over all the things that had happened today. The water was chilly but not freezing cold like in winter – the pipes in our apartment block had warmed up now it was spring. And the water inside the pipes too.

I wondered: could a real whale in an ocean somewhere get so hot in springtime that he would jump out of the water and just float up into the air, carefree? Or maybe it was something to do with global warming, like the bright yellow waves in my atlas? Would those waves get bigger and bigger, hotter and hotter, brighter and brighter? And then would all the whales and dolphins and sea mammals feel too hot and start living up in the open air, floating around in cities like shiny blimps? That would be so neat!

But how would the whale stop himself from falling down? I knew that the beluga whale is the smallest whale in the world. It weighs about 2,000 kilograms! That's twice as heavy as Dad's Toyota. His car needs an engine with the power of 135 horses to start it moving, so it would take way more horses to get it up in the air – that's why our car can't fly, Dad had explained. So how much horsepower does a flying whale need? The one I saw wasn't a beluga, so he's not even small. I was also pretty sure the whale didn't have an engine or propeller. Could a whale be hollow – just a super-light shell kept up in the air by warm winds like kites and birds with big wings? No – I knew that a whale couldn't be empty. People used to hunt them for their meat, and it meant that many whales were killed. So maybe he was a ghost whale? I didn't believe in ghosts, but I had to consider all the possibilities. The bath was half full when Mum interrupted my train of thought – and right when I felt I was close to cracking my mind-boggling scientific riddle! I hadn't even heard her coming home, but there she was, gently knocking on the bathroom door.

'Everything all right, Cappy?'

Cappy. I started getting called that after I lost my hair. Back in the hospital, I wore a knitted blue cap and decided that I'd never ever take it off. Mum hadn't let anyone touch my cap, not even when I was asleep or unconscious. '*Cappy, Cappy,*' the doctors and other mums and the volunteers and the nurses would say to me, then Mum started calling me that too.

'Everything's fine, Mum. No bruises!' I said cheerfully.

'That's good. So why don't you come out?' she asked, and I couldn't help but do just that.

Grandma had cooked dinner, the *boring* kind when we all have to have the same thing: the only kind of food I'm allowed to eat – boiled, bland, boring stuff. When we have a *normal* dinner, it's only me who gets the boring food: Mum and Grandma treat themselves. But a normal dinner also means that I'm lucky and can get something I crave: a slice of pizza, a baked apple, a piece of chocolate.

'I saw a whale,' I told Mum after dinner.

'On the internet?' she asked.

'No, here, in the park! A real whale!' I said, and then I blurted out, 'I swear!'

Grandma had told me that if someone said 'I swear!' it was obvious they wanted to fool you. Otherwise why would they take pains to assure you that you could trust them? But I said 'I swear!' all the time whenever I was worried. When I went to the hospital the first time, I said it hundreds of times, promising Mum I'd get better soon. Mum's training to become a set designer in Geneva had been about to start. I was meant to go with her and study at a French school, but we ended up in the hospital instead. Mum still took my French textbook along, even though it didn't make any sense to. I hadn't actually believed I would get better any time soon, but I said 'I swear!' anyway and kept repeating it, over and over, and that's how I realized Grandma was right.

'He was floating in the sky like a blimp, and then he plunged into the treetops,' I said. 'He must be hiding there now.' I paused. 'Can we go look for him? We'll come back in no time,' I added timidly, with no hope at all.

'DontbesillyCappy,' Mum said.

In one word, just like that. Like a tongue-twister.

Grandma gave her a hard look, but I knew why Mum had said that – she was worried, and she was busy thinking about her project. She's never been a careless mum – a little carefree, maybe – but having a carefree mum is great fun. If her project hadn't been on her mind, I'm sure she would have asked me more about the whale and where he might have come from. I could've told her a lot of facts and theories, and by bedtime we would've come up with a whole story about the whale. But tonight she only said:

'Take your pills, Cappy. Time for bed. I'll come and tuck you in, and then I've got work to do.'

Grandma gave me a wink, and I smiled back. Mum designs stuff for restaurants. Sometimes she makes forks with handles shaped like long fish,

or special plates – not round black and white ones, but curved and yellow and white like eggs cooked sunny side up. Sometimes she's not allowed to do that, so she spends a lot of time designing napkins, salt shakers, and serving boards for meat. She gets told that they should look normal, but not too boring; they should be nice, but not too nice; easy to use, but not like the things people usually have at home. You can never tell if clients are going to like Mum's ideas. If they don't, she has to start all over again. Mum must have the best imagination in the world. Grandma tells her all the time: 'You're just imagining things!' Grandma says that a lot, like she doesn't want her to imagine all kinds of things at once, I guess. She wants her to think up one new idea at a time – it's more fun like that.

After I brushed my teeth, Mum was waiting for me in the kitchen with a glass of water. I took the glass and three pills, and went to my room. I always take my pills by myself – I prefer to be alone because it's embarrassing to remember how I used to behave. Taking pills has become as easy as pie for me, but in the past I used to burst into tears and try to run away, and Mum would have to crush the pills and mix them in water, but then I'd find a way to spit the water out. Dad said I'd grown up over the past year, because I started taking the pills all by myself – I still keep my blue cap on, but I don't throw tantrums any more, or cry or demand anything. But I'm beginning to think that Dad isn't telling me the whole story. Growing up isn't just about doing things you don't like without saying anything. At least, it isn't just about that.

The night light was on in my room. I put the water and the pills on the bedside table and went over to the drawers to get my pyjamas, but I stopped halfway, shocked. There he was again! A huge whale by the window, his tail raised up, fins barely moving. He was hanging in the night sky, which was dotted with gleaming city lights, and he was looking through my window. One small round eye stared at me, while the other one, on the opposite side of his head, must have been watching the park and the sky above him. Then the whale swung round slowly to look at me with his other eye.

'Where did you come from?' I asked, opening the window and whispering so Mum wouldn't hear.

'I don't know,' the whale whispered back. 'You imagined me, I guess.'

'No way!' I said.

'I swear!' the whale said. And after a silence: 'I'm so hungry!'

'Sorry – I don't have anything to eat,' I said, embarrassed. I knew that whales filtered sea water and ate plankton, but I didn't have any sea water or plankton . . .

'Oh, yes, you do,' said the whale, interrupting my thoughts.

I knew right away what he was talking about. I took the pills and held my hand out of the window. The whale picked them up carefully with his soft, thick tongue, just like a pony. I even heard him smack his lips happily, breathing out of the blowhole at the top of his head. There were seashells and seaweed stuck to his skin. His fins were strong and firm, and his tail waved slowly up and down.

'Have you got a mum?' I asked, not really sure why.

'Nope,' the whale replied.

'What's it like – not having a mum?'

'It's OK. What it's like *having* a mum?'

'Having a mum is great!' I said.

We stayed silent for a minute or two.

'Got any more pills?' the whale asked sweetly.

'No,' I said. 'But I'll have some more tomorrow.'

'Why do you get to take pills every day?' the whale asked bluntly, but with a touch of envy.

'Because I've got leukaemia.'

'Oh, I see,' the whale said. 'See you tomorrow then.'

'See you,' I said, and then: 'Hey, hold on. Have you got a place to sleep?'

'*Pffft!*' The whale pushed the air out through his blowhole rudely and sank down to the treetops below.

He dropped down to the branches and swam off towards the park. The trees swayed ever so slightly in his wake, the leaves shimmering as they reflected the lights from the neighbours' windows. I watched until all became still again and then, after a while, called Mum to come and tuck me in.

Where Can You Buy a Mum and a Dad?

When I woke up in the morning, the whale was already there. He hovered over the park, spinning round and swishing his tail, scaring away birds and flies and small butterflies.

'See?' I said casually to Mum, when we sat down to breakfast, pointing at the whale through the window. Once she saw he was a real whale, she'd no longer be all *dontbesillyCappy*. That's for sure.

'It is a nice day today,' Mum said, slicing a loaf of bread. Just as she turned her head and swept her eyes over the park, the whale plunged down into the branches. 'It'll rain in the afternoon, though.'

I must have seemed worried, because she looked at me and asked, 'You don't want it to rain?'

I was staring through the window. The whale rose up out of the sea of leaves; he was floating over the park again.

'Can't see the rain, huh?' Mum followed my gaze. The whale vanished, quick as lightning. 'It's way up in the sky. It's still splashing around up there, but it'll fall soon.'

Mum was right – soft blue-grey clouds were piling up on the horizon beyond the park, like a whole pod of grumpy whales.

After breakfast, Mum gave me my pills, and I went to my room. Trying not to glance out of the window, I sat at my desk and spread the pills out on my palm. I looked at them as if they were super-delicious treats.

'Come on,' the whale outside the window murmured. 'Give them to me. Please.'

'No way,' I said, giving him a hard stare without blinking.

The whale pressed his flat grey forehead against the window. For some reason, I felt very sorry for him. 'Please, give them to me,' the whale begged me again. 'I'll show you the others.'

'What do you mean, *the others*?' I asked, confused.

'Others like me.'

I looked into his left eye, then into his right, trying to figure out if the whale was playing a trick on me. Finally, I opened the window and stretched out my hand. The whale slurped up the pills and gulped them down, happy.

'But not now,' he said. 'When the rain starts. Then we'll look up and see the others above the clouds.'

'You should say thank you,' I told the whale.

'Hmm,' he muttered. 'Why?'

'What do you mean, *why*?'

'Why should I say thank you?'

I gave it some thought. You thanked anyone who gave you a present or a treat, who helped you, who gave you advice or cheered you up. You were supposed to say thank you to the nurse who gave you a shot too, even though I found that hard to agree with.

'To do something good for someone who did something good for you,' I said at last, adding silently to myself: 'Or to someone who did something bad to you but for good reasons.'

'Thank you,' the whale said, then immediately asked, 'Do you feel good now?'

'I do,' I said.

'What if I keep saying thank you even if you don't give me anything – will you still feel good?'

'I guess.'

'Thank you,' the whale said.

We didn't say anything for a while. I was wondering whether praise you don't really deserve made you feel good. I decided that it didn't, but it felt good when someone wanted to do something good for me.

'Thank you,' I said too.

The whale nodded. He had learned his lesson in politeness.

'Where do you get your pills?' the whale asked.

'Mum buys them or gets them for me at the hospital.'

'So, to get pills, you have to have a mum,' the whale concluded.

'Or a dad,' I said. 'Dad buys pills for me too. Or gets them at the hospital.'

'I see. And where can you buy a mum or a dad?' the whale asked. 'Or can you get them at the hospital too?'

'I had a mum and a dad from day one,' I said. 'Or they had me, I guess. We lived together, all three of us. We just got given to each other.'

'But *who* gave you to each other?' The whale was trying hard to understand.

'Someone who decides things about people. Someone who thinks that they'll feel good, safe and happy together,' I went on, not really clear myself who that someone was who had given me to my mum and dad, and my mum and dad to me. 'But later Mum gave Dad back.'

'Back to who?' the whale persisted.

'I don't know,' I admitted. 'I have Dad, but Mum doesn't. We got Grandma instead, though! I mean, she was there in the past too, but not really with us. But now she's living here.'

'Does she bring pills too?' the whale asked.

'Grandma does tons of other good things,' I said. 'She works at the library and brings home paper and pencils for me. She knows all the best books in the world and takes me to the park where I can play with dogs. But I'm not supposed to tell Mum about that, because I might get some disease and then I'll never get better. If I hadn't got sick, they would've bought me a dog or a cat, for sure. I'd like a dog more, of course.'

'A dog or a cat,' the whale repeated. Then he asked, 'Would you eat them?'

'*Eat them?* No! I'd love them!'

'But you love them anyway,' the whale said. 'So you already got what you want.'

'Dogs are friendly and cuddly. Cats are soft and gentle. You can play with them. They sleep on your bed and snuggle with you and scratch chairs and sofas, and they treat you like a friend,' I said. 'If you want to feel good but don't know how, you should just get a dog or cat and love it.'

'You can love it even if you don't have it, though, if that's what's important,' the whale said.

I thought about Dad, who I really love, and about the swimming pool, which I love too, even though I can't go there any more. And about that school where I didn't start after all, even though I love reading and watching movies about school, daydreaming about the day I'll finally get to go there. (Grandma said the reason I loved that school so much was that I'd never had to go there!) I thought about my coach. And about Mum, who designs forks and cutting boards, even though she loves designing stage sets best of all.

'Yes, you can,' I agreed. 'And that's important, yes.'

'Cappy!'

I turned round when Mum called me from the living room. When I looked back out of the window, there were only clouds in the sky.

Mum and I did my vitamin vapours and then Mum did the dishes while I told her about the right way to treat my illness. I'd read about it in a book – the first one they'd given me at the hospital. I liked the way it explained that there is a monster called Leukaemia living in my blood and told me how to fight it and not to die. I knew right away, of course, that it was a book for little kids and that leukaemia is not a monster but a disease. The book was still great, even though it didn't tell me about the 'dying' bit. I figured that out by myself.

When someone died at the hospital, their mums and grandmas left quickly, and my mum cried. No one wanted to take over the beds of anyone whose family had left the hospital that quickly, so we'd trick the newcomers.

'It was Denys's bed,' we'd say. 'But he got well and left. That one was Kristina's, but she went home.'

'It's not OK to lie,' Mum had said. 'But sometimes you just have to.'

The hospital book didn't say anything about this, so I decided that while I

couldn't learn everything from books, I should never ever forget the things I did learn from it. Mum checked that every day.

'What's the most important rule?' she asked me.

'To have no fear!' I said.

'What else?'

'To be good.'

I had no trouble with the first rule. The second one was trickier.

As the morning went on, the park got covered in clouds. The rain was splashing inside them so loudly that I could almost hear heavy raindrops rubbing against one another, as if trying to burst the cloud's thin, tight skin.

Mum and I did my homework: she drew all kinds of things, and I had to write what each of them was. She drew a house, and I wrote 'HOUSE'; she drew a froggy, and I wrote 'FROG', because it's shorter that way. Then Mum drew a puppy, and I wrote 'LOVE'. Mum smiled and drew herself, wearing her glasses, old shirt and slippers. I wrote 'LOVE' again – this time my letters were so huge that I needed another sheet of paper. Then we had lunch, and I went to my room for a nap. But I wasn't going to sleep, of course.

I climbed into my bed, burying my head under the blanket, so I wouldn't sneak a look at the window to see if the rain had started. I knew that if you sneaked a peek at the kettle while waiting for it to boil, it would take at least twice as long, and if you peeked at the oven, curious when the plum pie would be ready, it would take forever to bake. That's why I kept quiet, but I was all ears. Suddenly something snapped and there was a loud noise, as if someone had ripped apart a strong pillowcase or an old bed sheet. The rain, restless, spilled out of the cloud.

Others Above the Clouds

'Are you coming or what?' the whale asked, hovering outside the window.

Rain was streaming down his skin, tumbling against the seaweeds and shells.

Standing in front of the window, I looked at the whale. Glossy and wet, he turned bright blue, like my cap. The whale opened and closed his large mouth, sipping the rainwater, a jet of vapour coming out of his blowhole.

'It's not cold,' he said, trying to encourage me.

I knew it wasn't cold – I'd figured that out by myself. But it *was* way too wet. I quickly came up with an idea.

I dug my swimming trunks out of the wardrobe, then a swimming cap and goggles. I was sure I'd feel better in the rain if I had my swimming gear on. Thinking about it some more, I took my blue cap out of a drawer – I felt safer that way – and I pulled it on over the swimming cap.

I climbed on my desk and opened the window. The rain, swishing and tingling, dashed inside the room, splashing on my feet and shoulders. The whale moved closer, right up to the windowsill.

'Climb up,' he said. And I did – I climbed out of the window and on to his huge back.

The whale was a tad slippery, like cliffs by the sea, wet from salty waves. He was warm, though, full of a special whale warmth – just as I imagined he would be if I touched him. I grabbed the bumps on his back, and we floated away.

The shiny park below was rustling with raindrops tapping on curly leaves, jumping from one leaf to another. Passers-by were hiding under the branches. The trees scooped up the water with their cupped leaves and were trying to pick who should get wet and who would be lucky to come out dry, just like mischievous kids hiding with a plastic bottle of water on a balcony overlooking the street. Oh, I knew very well how such things were done.

Then we flew over the city. Its wet roofs were reddish, glistening black or dark green, the streets empty. From time to time, someone would run across the road from their car to their home or to a cafe, covering their heads with a bag or a magazine. From above, the running figures looked so tiny and funny. I wanted to hover over the city for a long, long time, peering into the courtyards and playgrounds, deserted school yards and tennis courts near the park, but the whale said, 'We have to get higher.'

He started to rise. His blowhole grunted softly, as if he was rising out of the ocean depths, eager to take a breath.

Reaching the very top of the rain, we dived into the grey clouds, which were thick like down in a tightly stuffed pillow, or like toy filling. It was so hazy around me that I could hardly see anything – I could only hear heavy raindrops pelting down, one after another. I was soaked through; my blue cap didn't have a dry thread and it clung to the swimming cap underneath. The water dripped down behind my ears and on to my back.

All of a sudden I was dazzled.

When I could finally open my eyes, I realized where all the sunlight hides on rainy, gloomy days. The whale was floating above the thick grey cloud that blotted out the entire city below. We were surrounded by endless blue and overflowing sunlight – I'd never seen anything so shiny.

'Wow, it's so sunny here!' I said.

'Oh, come on,' the whale said sniffily. 'Don't tell me you've never been on an aeroplane.'

But I hadn't. I had never seen so much sunlight before either.

The sun quickly made me dry and warm. I was just about to doze off on the whale's nice, sun-warmed back, when he said, 'Well, here's a bear for you.'

A bear? I looked around – and there it was.

The bear was huge. It was white with a wide black nose, and heavy and clumsy. I watched, wide-eyed, as it rolled on its back in the sky, trying to catch sunbeams with its paws, whuffing happily.

The whale glided closer.

'At night, when the lights go out, it climbs through a window into a room and hugs a little girl. She cuddles up to its soft belly and falls asleep,' the whale said. 'I think her name is Sasha. Look how large the bear is – it can barely squeeze through the window.'

'No way!' I cried. I wish I had a sleeping bear like that!

'Upon my word!' the whale said, and then he added, as if sensing something, 'The bear didn't take her up here.'

Next, we saw a sad red dragon swimming over the clouds. It looked bored – the whale said the parents of the twins who were its friends didn't allow them to go out in the rain.

'Once, this dragon breathed fire into their electric heater,' the whale said. 'So now, if you turn it on, the heater glows red and hot dragon's breath warms up their bedroom. The kids cracked that secret and became friends with the dragon.'

We saw a ship too – a giant sailing boat, sleek with its sails puffed up, crisp white like a festive day.

'One boy used to play with it,' the whale said. 'But it was much smaller back then, just a little boat that could take you to the stars on a moonlit night. The boy grew up and gave his boat to his younger sister. All of a sudden, the boat shot up, like a sapling in good soil, bursting into blossom with its white sails. In fine weather, bells tinkle on its masts. But the girl is too little to sail. She just watches it all day long and comes up with melodies for its bells. One day she'll set sail, though. That's for sure.'

All the creatures were hiding from the rain, rising over it, bored without their little friends. A few spaceships that belonged to a group of classmates were racing along the horizon. A snow-white horse with a rainbow mane was

taking careful steps, lower and lower, until it could graze on the grey cloud as if it were the pasture. A chubby sheep with silver bells on its neck munched on the cloud next to it. There was another horse – dark, huge, with strong, black wings and in a harness. It looked back anxiously at its empty saddle, waiting for a restless little rider. A bunch of white butterflies fluttered around us and flew high up to a small nodding head of a giant brachiosaurus. A fox, bright red and as large as the setting sun, stretched out on the horizon, wagging its long shiny tail. A panda, soft as a feather – and as big as my bedroom – was sleeping warily, curled up in a ball like a cat.

'They all belong to someone?' I asked, bright-eyed.

'You bet they do,' the whale said. 'All of us in this world belong to someone, you know.'

I knew it was true.

After a while, the whale said, 'We have to go back. The rain is almost over. The cloud is petering out. See?'

I looked down. The whale was right: the cloud was thinning out as if the horses and the sheep in the sky had chomped large patches out of it. You could see the city with its streets, roofs and trees down below.

'Listen to me,' the whale said, sinking deeper and deeper into the cloud. 'When you get home, take a towel from the bathroom, dry yourself and then dry off your swimming cap and goggles. But don't throw them on the floor –

put them back in your wardrobe. Then spread your swimming trunks and the blue cap on the windowsill. After the rain, the sun will come out and dry them.'

When the whale reached my window, the clouds had almost drifted away. Sitting on the whale's back, I hung my legs over one side, ready to jump on to the windowsill – right through the open window.

'Would you like a seashell?' the whale asked as I landed on my desk.

'Yes!' I cried.

'Go ahead and take one.'

Among the seashells stuck to his back, I chose a small delicate pink one and picked it off gently, as if it had climbed on to my palm by itself.

Back in my room, I did exactly as the whale said. The moment I spread my wet swimming trunks and blue cap on the windowsill, the sun poked through the clouds, the bright sunshine pouring down on to the city just as the shower had a few minutes ago.

A List of Very Sad Things

It rained again, pouring all day long, and it did the next day, and the next. Grandma took a taxi to get to work. Mum didn't go out anywhere; she sat in front of her laptop all day, thinking, designing, drawing and then drawing some more. She had a midnight deadline. At night, some mammals – predators and monkeys – and small rodents come out; the owl hunts; photosynthesis slows down – and Mum turns in her projects. That's how the world works.

I did French exercises on my tablet and watched a video about sailing, and then I began to wait. Recently, I'd realized that I actually enjoyed waiting. At the hospital, I hated waiting – waiting until they gave me a shot, until they took me for a scary, painful blood test, until they told me if I'd got a tiny bit better compared to the previous day; waiting to see if Mum would cry after the doctor's check-up. It was especially hard to wait until Dad or Grandma visited, because I knew they'd leave again pretty soon.

But nowadays I was usually waiting for Mum to finish her work and think up something specially for me; waiting for when I could take my pills back to my room and talk to and play with the whale; waiting for Grandma to bring me new

31

books, pencils and felt-tip pens. All the waiting was now full of daydreaming, full of joy – in my fantasies, things happened just the way I wanted them to. I was waiting until I got well and went to school; until I could fly to the beach with Mum; until I could play with my friends and a bunch of dogs in the park for as long as I wanted to. I was waiting until I would be tall enough to reach the pedals in Dad's Toyota; until I grew up and earned lots of money. All those things that simply had to happen in the future, they filled my days with light – just like the lights of cars seen way off across the park filled my dark room with their soft glow. If I couldn't sleep at night, I would wait for those lights. Once, Mum and I sat together like that almost all night long in the living room – spots of light sweeping over us, long shadows twisting our faces, stretching out our noses and mouths, making our eyes bulge. We burst out laughing each time a car passed, until Grandma came and shooed us away to sleep.

When it was four o'clock in the afternoon, Dad opened the door with his key.

'Ihor,' Mum said when she heard him coming. 'Take off your shoes, please.'

Dad took off his Converse trainers and came into my room. He always takes off his shoes the way you shouldn't do – he doesn't untie his shoelaces, but steps with one shoe on the heel of the other one, pulling it off.

'Well?' he said.

I ran to him, laughing, and before Mum came in we did the things we always did: I jumped into his arms, and he turned me upside down, grabbing my ankles, and spun me round, and then turned me the right way up and threw me in the air a couple of times.

'Hey, Cappy, you're not fat any more,' Dad said, smiling.

Dad was very sad when I ballooned up after all those pills. I guess it was because it was too hard for him to spin me round and throw me in the air. I haven't been fat for quite a while now, ever since I've come home from the hospital, in fact, but for some reason Dad said that to me every week, again and again, as it were a great discovery. As if he was trying to convince himself that I'd slimmed down for real and that pills would never ever make me fat again.

'You won't forget anything, will you, Ihor?' Mum asked Dad after she said hi and gave him a quick hug. 'Eight people inside, tops. No dairy. Ice cream has milk in it too . . .'

'No running, because he has too little calcium in his bones. No raw, fried or fatty foods. No toys he doesn't really need. No dogs. And as much fresh air as possible,' Dad and I chimed in.

Later that evening, I told the whale about our day. It was a different story from the one I told Mum. I didn't lie to her, not quite; it's just that she doesn't really need to know that Dad bought a large roll of cling film and wrapped me in it like a mummy, leaving only a gap for my face, so my clothes wouldn't get wet while we played football in the rain on an empty football pitch. How could I explain it to her that a longboard that I can't ride yet, and flippers that I have nowhere to use right now are not 'toys I don't really need' but an important investment into my future? And that the clumsy puppy Dad's friends let me hold wouldn't have made any difference anyway – at that moment, I had still been wrapped in cling film.

Dad sends all the pictures that Mum shouldn't see – like the one with me looking like a mummy or sitting on a Central Asian shepherd dog – to our secret email account. The stuff I shouldn't show Mum for now, he stacks in a box in the back of his Toyota. When I finally get better, I'll put all the things I might need in that box too.

'Does your dad put pills in that box as well?' the whale asked – I wonder whether he was thinking of tracking down Dad's Toyota.

'No, he gives them to Mum right away,' I said.

'Hmm, it's weird,' the whale said. 'Your dad was so sad when he left tonight. And your mum was sad. And you were sad too. You got the pills, but everyone is sad. Why? I don't get it.'

'Mum is sad because she and Dad didn't make it,' I explained. 'Sometimes she says they could have made it. That's when Grandma tells her that she's just imagining things.'

'What is it that they didn't make?' the whale asked.

'I don't know,' I admitted. 'Something or other. But it makes all three of us very sad.'

'Do they give you pills even when you're sad?' the whale asked, just in case.

'They do,' I replied.

'OK. See you in the morning then,' he said, sounding relieved, and he vanished into the darkness outside. My sadness didn't vanish, though.

It was time for bed, but I couldn't get rid of that sadness. It touched me on the inside, and it was an OK feeling, really – I didn't feel any pain, but I also couldn't fall asleep while it was there. They had told me at the hospital that I should tell them about anything that scared me or stopped me from doing things, and I did what they said – I told a special doctor all about it and I felt better. Mum had also talked to her. I could tell things like this to Grandma or Mum, but what if my sadness jumped to them? So I grabbed my tablet and started to make a list of very sad things as though I was telling myself about them:

A List of Very Sad Things:
1. That Mum and Dad didn't make it.
2. When someone carries a pet travel box in the street, but the box is empty and there is no dog or even a cat inside.

I don't know why, but I couldn't think of anything else. I knew lots of sad and scary things: things that I'd seen or been through at the hospital, but they'd slipped my mind, like those French words that I learned – *really* learned – in the evening but couldn't remember in the morning when Mum checked them. So that's what I wrote down next:

3. When you forget good and happy things as quickly as bad things.

I thought that must be very, very sad, even though it has never happened to me. And then I fell asleep.

WHAT TO DO WITH
WHAT YOU'VE GOT

I got used to having the whale around. I asked him a couple of times if I could show him to Mum and Grandma or at least to Dad – he wouldn't tell anyone, for sure. You should always share the best things you have, I said. And the whale really was the best – so kind and huge. But the whale's argument was very simple: only the one who's got the pills gets to play with the whale. He would circle above the park in front of my window all day long, but as soon as Mum or Grandma glanced out he would vanish into the clouds or the green treetops or he would dash far, far away, turning into a tiny black dot, like a pigeon or a crow – a distant secret that you couldn't look at up close. But I didn't lose hope that I would talk him into it somehow. My point was that Mum and Dad had a direct connection to the pills I, or rather he, took.

I asked Mum once: 'Those pills I'm taking – who do they belong to?'

'To you,' Mum said, surprised.

'But it's you or Dad who gets them. Or someone at the hospital.'

'The pills are yours and they help you,' Mum said. Thinking for a bit, she added, 'In fact, everything that Dad and I buy or have belongs to you too.'

'Even your car?' I couldn't believe it. 'And Dad's?'

'Sure,' Mum said.

'Even Dad's paintball gun? And your phone? And your snowboard? And all your money? And Dad's money?' I held my breath.

'Well, yes.'

I let my breath out. 'Why didn't you tell me that earlier?'

'I'm telling you now,' Mum said. 'But does it change anything?'

I thought about it. It was so great to know that all of a sudden I had so much stuff, but Mum was right – it didn't really change anything. Dad's paintball gun and Mum's snowboard were too big for me, but, even if they weren't, I couldn't use either of them yet. I could have piled extra toys into Mum's car, of course, but then they would have got dirty, which is dangerous for me, and then I would have had to throw them away. As a car owner, I could have told Dad that from now on I'd sit in the front passenger seat, but then the police would have stopped us over and over and we wouldn't have got anywhere. I could have bought all kinds of things with Mum's and Dad's money, but they would probably have been things I don't need yet. And anyway Mum and Dad buy everything that I could want and that I need.

'So . . . does it?' Mum asked.

'No – it doesn't change anything,' I said, and then suddenly realized something. 'So, when I took your phone to the park last winter and lost it, does that mean I lost my own phone?'

'Well, it looks that way,' Mum said.

What a shame.

'And your new phone – is it mine too?' I asked.

'It is,' Mum said.

'But I should ask you first before I can take it, right?' I wanted to be clear.

'You should,' Mum said. 'See how smart you are, Cappy? You figured everything out by yourself.'

Actually, I hadn't figured out that much – I only knew now that I have a whole bunch of stuff I can't use yet. So a bit later I went over to Mum and asked, 'And what about all your things, Mum? Are they mine, just like they're yours, or a bit more yours than mine?'

'Everything's yours,' Mum said. 'All yours. But please keep in mind that as your things are also mine, I don't like to see them broken, lost, dirty or scattered around, OK? I need my things, and sometimes our good life – yours and mine – depends on them. They belong to you, just as I said, but that means something else too.'

'That I have to take care of them?'

'You got it,' Mum said. 'You should take care of them as if they were yours.'

In the evening, I told the whale about that conversation I had with Mum. He got really excited.

'If all that stuff is yours, can you take it and swap it for pills?' he wondered.

'I don't think Mum and Dad will agree to that,' I said. 'And I don't need so many pills anyway.'

'You're thinking only about yourself,' the whale said, slurping up the colourful pills from my palm. 'And you've dozens of people thinking about you.'

'But I think about you too,' I said.

'Do you really?' the whale asked.

'I do.' I suddenly felt sorry for him, because it sounded like no one else was thinking about him – only me.

'Do you have no one else in your life?' I asked.

'What do you mean, *no one else*?' the whale replied, sounding a bit annoyed by my question. 'Sure, I do. Come here – see for yourself.'

I climbed on to the windowsill and the whale floated right next to me. I jumped on to his giant back, taking a few cautious steps between the tufts of old seaweed and clusters of seashells.

'Hey! Be careful,' the whale snapped.

I looked closer at his back and saw two shiny black dots. They turned out to be the scared eyes of a little bird. It was really tiny and grey.

'Oh, wow!' I gasped.

The bird had made a neat little nest among the seaweed and seashells.

'Don't touch her,' the whale warned me.

Trying not to lose balance on the whale's back, I kneeled down beside the bird and her nest. The bird chirped loudly a couple of times and then calmed down. I crouched like that for some time, and she seemed to forget about my presence. She started to peck at the seaweed and then flitted upwards to chase a mosquito hovering over my head, but she came back right away – and that's when I spotted two tiny eggs, grey with blue and yellow dots, lying in the nest.

'What's it like?' the whale asked. 'I can't see the nest.'

'There're nice little eggs in the nest,' I said.

'How little?' he asked.

'Tiny,' I said.

'This is what happens when you sleep among the leaves in the park,' the whale said happily.

I sat on his back for a while. It was so nice and warm. The bird must have been very comfortable there.

'What will you do with them?' I asked.

'Dunno,' the whale said. 'I'll take care of them, I guess. Right?'

'Right,' I said. 'You have to take care of what you got.'

Mum and I Go Sailing

Rainy days were followed by warm and sunny ones, and I spent lots of time outside with my family: in the park with Mum and Grandma, or in all kinds of places with Dad. At first, Mum stopped worrying – her project had been accepted and she had plenty of free time at last. I taught her how to draw a whale with a nest on his back. Two bald pink birdies were squeaking in the nest now, and the little grey bird was hunting for insects all day long to feed them. Once, I noticed that there were, in fact, two little grey birds and that they were taking turns.

'It's so great to have not just three but *four* birds instead of one!' the whale cheered.

'It's so great to have such a lively imagination! A whale floating above the park and birds nesting on his back – Cappy, you're really creative!' Mum said, surprised.

But then we all got worried. Mum was first, of course. One morning I came into the kitchen and saw her with blue-black tears on her cheeks. I heard Grandma telling her, 'You're just imagining things,' but this time she said it in an unusual way, gentle and soft. Mum washed her face and cheered up, but after lunch I got a whole baked apple, and that meant for sure that something was wrong.

'I can't quite figure out what's going on,' I told the whale before bedtime.

He squinted, trying to catch a glimpse of the baby birdies on his back that kept chirping, asking for food, night and day.

'No one gives out forbidden treats to sick boys just like that,' I said, thinking out loud. 'After I left the hospital, I was allowed to eat only one little slice of apple. So a whole apple . . . That's weird.'

'Why not ask them?' the whale suggested. 'I would do that if I were you. Did you get the pills, by the way?'

I reached out my hand. Little grey birds circled over my palm, but they didn't seem interested. The whale slurped up the pills and sucked them in, making a funny sound.

In the morning, I asked Mum over breakfast, 'Why did you give me a whole baked apple yesterday when I'm not allowed to eat that much?'

I regretted asking right away, because Mum started to shrink before my eyes, and I knew she was about to burst into tears.

'Cappy,' Grandma said. 'At the end of this week, you have to go back into hospital. The protocol is almost over.'

Oh no, it had completely slipped my mind. The 'protocol' Grandma was talking about is a treatment that takes an exact number of days until it comes to an end. Back at the hospital, I used to try to count the days of the protocol, but there were too many of them and I gave up. At home, where I didn't have to do anything but take my pills, I forgot all about it. Every week, a hospital nurse came to take my blood, but I'd become so used to it that I no longer paid attention to her. Each time, she said that I was a brave boy and that I was getting better. Nothing interesting, because I knew that much myself.

But whenever a protocol finishes, I have to go to hospital where they would tell me whether I really have got better. 'Really getting better' is not the same as 'getting better' little by little every day. I always have to do a lot of tests, and I don't like them at all, but I can sit still and I'm not afraid, and that was all that I have to do. This time, though, I knew I could sit still, but I wasn't so sure that I wouldn't be afraid.

'You really are better,' Mum said. 'I sw–' She stopped short and looked at me helplessly.

Dad and I spent the next day driving. I was still too small to hold the wheel and press the pedals at the same time, but Dad put me on his lap and I steered the car while he pressed everything he needed to press. I only did that for a bit, of course, when no one was looking. That day, I put new things into my box – a collar and a leash for a real dog, and it was almost as nice as having a dog, because if you have a collar, you will definitely have a dog to put it on some day.

In the evening, when we got back home, Mum and Dad shut themselves in the kitchen and talked for a long time.

'Do they make it?' I asked Grandma.

'Make what?' she said, confused, and then added, just in case, 'You're just imagining things!'

The whale couldn't understand why I wasn't happy about going to the hospital. You'll hear good news either way, he said. If I really had got better, great; if not, I'd get lots of new pills and really get better afterwards. I didn't quite agree with the whale, but I felt better talking with him through the open window and listening to the birdies chirping.

The next morning, when we had to go to the hospital, it turned out that it had started raining during the night and that the rain wasn't planning to stop for another thousand days – it was that heavy. We packed my tablet, the pills, all the things I needed, my pyjamas and my blue knitted cap, and Grandma took an umbrella and walked with us to the car.

Mum drove me to the hospital, turning from our little street to a bigger one, then to another one, even bigger. She was silent the whole time, then suddenly she couldn't help but smile – the biggest street we had to take was full of water, from side to side! Just like a river. Cars paddled through it, splashing water all around.

'We're sailing, Cappy,' Mum said.

I started to laugh. She laughed too. Fountains were rising on both sides of our car, as if a pod of whales was keeping us company.

I felt so calm, sailing through the rain together with Mum, like in a boat.

I even started to dream that we would drift forever and that the rain falling all around our car would become a wall between our cosy little world, warmed up by the car heater, and everything else. There were no adventures, no whale, no Grandma or Dad, no birdies, no dogs and no swimming pool in this world, but there weren't any diseases, tests, fear, pain or even sadness there either.

I'd made up my mind too soon about adventures, though, because at the next traffic lights, Mum started to slow down and said that our boat needed to follow the navigation signals. The bumper of a big black shiny car, invisible in all that rain, appeared right in front of us, and our boat poked its nose into it, slowly and helplessly.

It was a real car accident. I was delighted.

'Wow!' I cried. 'That was so cool!'

But Mum obviously thought differently. She turned on the hazard lights and jumped out of the car. Through the wet windscreen, I could see a man get out of the black car. He stood in the rain while my mum talked and talked, her shoulders trembling. It took quite a while. The man took off his soaked jacket, as if it would be any use by that time. He draped it over Mum's shoulders and hugged her. They stood like that in the pouring rain – Mum and a stranger whose car we'd just smashed.

Then Mum came back. This time she climbed into the passenger seat in front of me.

'Everything's OK, Cappy?' she asked, as if it were me who was soaked in the rain or had all the make-up in the world smudged on my face. 'I know you got scared.'

'I didn't,' I said.

All of a sudden, the soaked man from the black car opened the door and sat in the driver's seat, moving it back as far as possible. He had moved his black car, but I couldn't see where it was in all that rain.

'Hey there,' he said.

'Hello,' I said politely. 'Are you a drowned rat?'

'Cappy!' Mum gasped, round-eyed.

The man laughed. 'A drowned rat? Why?'

'When someone gets wet, Grandma says they're like a drowned rat. I've never seen anyone as wet as you are now, only in the swimming pool. So, you aren't a drowned rat?'

'I'm afraid not,' the man said. 'Sorry for disappointing you.'

We went to the hospital, the three of us: Mum, Mr Drowned Rat and me. I think that the stranger was a rat who'd drowned in that rain and had turned into a man, even though he said he wasn't. It was the first time I'd seen someone like that.

Far above the rain, the whale was making his birdies warm in the bright sun. I knew that he was trying to look through the cloud to see how things were going with me.

Soon Things Would Be So Great

On our way back home, I thought that it hadn't been as bad at the hospital as it had seemed when I was there half an hour ago. I have no idea how it works but, as time goes by, things that happened in the past always seem better and easier. This time, I almost immediately forgot that I'd just spent one day and one night at the hospital. When we arrived home, Mr Drowned Rat picked me up in his arms and took me to our apartment upstairs.

'Who's that?' Grandma whispered.

'Oh,' Mum said with a little sigh. 'Later.'

'*Mr Drowned Rat*,' I said to Grandma as quietly as possible.

'That much I can see,' Grandma huffed, and went to the kitchen. I have no idea how she could have seen that, because Mr Drowned Rat had changed his clothes since yesterday and was now completely dry.

I knew that Mr Drowned Rat stayed with Mum at the hospital almost the whole time. I slept during check-ups and I also dozed off and woke up, again and again, in the ward. Once I even heard Mum laughing somewhere in the corridor. When I finally woke up properly, Mum sat beside me and didn't go anywhere. I could see his black car parked outside by Mum's white car.

Mr Drowned Rat gently patted me on the head, said goodbye and left. I quite liked him, Mr Drowned Rat, and he had a nice big car, even though Mum and I had damaged it a bit.

'Well timed,' Grandma grumbled, but Mum didn't say anything.

When Mr Drowned Rat went home, Mum sat on my bed, took off my blue knitted cap and asked, 'Are you scared, Cappy?'

But I wasn't scared. I was back home, the sun was shining above the park, Grandma was murmuring in the kitchen, and Mum was hugging me, her arms so warm.

'I'll stay with you for a while, then I'll go to the hospital and find out how things are,' Mum said. 'I could call them, but it would be faster just to go there.'

'Is Mr Drowned Rat giving you a lift?' I asked.

'Dad is,' Mum said. 'That's what we agreed. He's so worried.'

'I got better,' I told her. I'd been good and brave for so long that I even forgot to add 'I swear'. Mum stretched out on the bed beside me, stroking my hair, and then her eyes closed and she dozed off.

The whale was hovering outside the window, chewing his lips to show how terrible and unfair it had been that I couldn't open the window at the hospital and feed him pills.

I looked at his eyes. He seemed to be thinking, 'Grey birds feed their little birdies day and night, and look what you did.'

I wanted to wave at him, to show that I hadn't stopped thinking about him,

but then Mum woke up. She looked at me for a long time, and then she left, gently closing the door behind her. She didn't even look out of the window. The whale followed her with his eyes.

'You will still live in the park, even if I get better, won't you?' I asked.

'I will,' the whale said. 'And you will feed me some other pills, vitamins, won't you?'

'I will,' I replied, nodding. 'Summer will be over soon, and then your birdies will grow up.'

'I know,' the whale said. 'Some day you'll grow up too.'

'But first I'll go to school,' I said. 'And I think that will take a while, so don't worry.'

'Would you like to sneak a peek?' the whale asked all of a sudden.

Of course, I wanted to! The whale's warm back was really wide and soft. Carefully, so as not to scare away the birdies, we floated away over the park and above the city. I pointed out my swimming pool that I'll return to very soon; we glided over a school that I might go to – or maybe this one, not that. And there's the huge car park behind the supermarket where Dad will teach me to drive his Toyota. We went past Grandma's library that I'll be visiting again soon; streets where I'll ride my longboard; coffee houses where Mum and I will eat ice cream; kids who will become my friends – all coming up this summer, which will turn into sunny autumn and cold, snowy winter. There are all kinds of fun things and adventures I've been looking forward to.

It was worth doing my best to be brave and good for so long to get all these things. I decided that I'll do that in the future too – just in case. And then I looked down and saw swings and sandpits below, sports grounds and rooftop terraces, funny-looking fountains in the squares and tramlines with striped trams crawling along them like snails, gardens with tiny sour apricots and yellow plums, a stadium and the black car that belongs to Mr Drowned Rat; just like us, he came to the hospital to sneak a peek. He won't talk to my mum once she comes out, but he'll see her face and understand everything.

The whale made a few circles above the hospital. Through one of the windows, we saw Mum and Dad sitting on a windowsill in front of a white door, silent and holding hands – not like people who've fallen in love but like two scared kids. I wanted to shout to them that soon things would be so great, but I didn't want to scare the birdies.

It's all right, though. Mum and Dad can wait a bit, then learn everything for themselves.

PUFFIN BOOKS

UK | USA | Canada | Ireland | Australia
India | New Zealand | South Africa

Puffin Books is part of the Penguin Random House group of companies
whose addresses can be found at global.penguinrandomhouse.com.

www.penguin.co.uk   www.puffin.co.uk   www.ladybird.co.uk

First published in Ukraine by Old Lion Publishing House 2015
This English-language edition published in Great Britain by Puffin Books 2022

001

Typeset in Amatic and Gothic A1
Printed and bound in Italy

The authorized representative in the EEA is Penguin Random House Ireland,
Morrison Chambers, 32 Nassau Street, Dublin D02 YH68

A CIP catalogue record for this book is available from the British Library

ISBN: 978-0-241-61542-3

All correspondence to:
Puffin Books, Penguin Random House Children's
One Embassy Gardens, 8 Viaduct Gardens, London SW11 7BW